Holly Smale is the author of *Geek Girl*, *Model Misfit*, *Picture Perfect*, *All that Glitters*, *Head Over Heels* and *Geek Girl* novellas, *All Wrapped Up* and *Sunny Side Up*. She was unexpectedly spotted by a top London modelling agency at the age of fifteen and spent the following two years falling over on catwalks, going bright red and breaking things she couldn't afford to replace. By the time Holly had graduated from Bristol University with a BA in English Literature and an MA in Shakespeare she had given up modelling and set herself on the path to becoming a writer.

Geek Girl was the no. 1 bestselling young adult fiction title in the UK in 2013. It was shortlisted for several major awards and won the Teen and Young Adult category of the Waterstones Children's Book Prize. The series has been published in 28 languages all over the world. Holly is currently writing the sixth and final book in the *Geek Girl* series.

Follow Holly Smale on Twitter and Instagram:
@holsmale
www.facebook.com/geekgirlseries

*For all my geek girls and boys,
wherever you are.*

Merry Christmas.

GEEK GIRL

ALL
WRAPPED UP

HOLLY
SMALE

HarperCollins *Children's Books*

First published in Great Britain by HarperCollins *Children's Books* in 2015
This paperback edition first published in Great Britain by HarperCollins
Children's Books in 2016
HarperCollins *Children's Books* is a division of HarperCollins*Publishers* Ltd,
HarperCollins Publishers
1 London Bridge Street
London SE1 9GF

The HarperCollins website address is: www.harpercollins.co.uk

1

Copyright © Holly Smale 2015

ISBN 978–0–00–819544–1

Holly Smale asserts the moral right to be identified as the author of the work.

Typeset by Palimpsest Book Production Limited, Falkirk, Stirlingshire
Printed and bound in England by Clays Ltd, St Ives plc

MIX
Paper from
responsible sources
FSC™ C007454

FSC™ is a non-profit international organisation established to promote
the responsible management of the world's forests. Products carrying the
FSC label are independently certified to assure consumers that they come
from forests that are managed to meet the social, economic and
ecological needs of present and future generations,
and other controlled sources.

Find out more about HarperCollins and the environment at
www.harpercollins.co.uk/green

celebrate [cel-e-brate] verb

1 To observe or commemorate an event

2 To mark with festivities

3 To proclaim or make public

4 To praise widely

5 To perform appropriate rites and ceremonies

ORIGIN from the Latin *celebrare* – to honour

1

My name is Harriet Manners, and I love Christmas.

You can tell I love Christmas because I start celebrating it in the middle of August.

I do it subtly, obviously.

A tinsel brooch here, a life-size plastic reindeer with flashing nose there.

"*Harriet,*" my stepmother said this year when I wheeled it into the hallway.

"*Annabel*," I replied, making my face as angelic as possible. "Did you know that the majority of male reindeers lose their antlers in winter? That means that Rudolph was almost definitely a girl. Don't you think we should be reminded of this *every day of the year*?"

Annabel laughed and put the reindeer back in the garden shed, along with my 'Jingle Cat – Meowy Christmas' album and the cinnamon incense sticks I'd hidden behind the radiators.

So I think the answer was no.

In September I constructed a battle of pink versus white sugar mice on the living room carpet, and October was spent sticking thick wads of cotton wool along the edge of every external windowsill so it looked like it had just been snowing.

"*Harriet*," Annabel repeated, which means November was spent cleaning it all off again.

Now it's the middle of December and I'm finally *allowed* to start marking the occasion, I'm so excited I feel like a shaken can: except instead of soda, Christmas is fizzing straight out.

I have made a neat list of my favourite Christmas animals, and my favourite Christmas foods, and my favourite Christmas songs, and my favourite Christmas lists.

I've created a gift plan with associated shopping map, and a detailed Q and A to hand out on Christmas morning so I can accurately deduce how much people *really* like their presents.

Together, my best friend and I found a

traditional mince pie recipe from a Tudor recipe book written in 1543 and cooked them perfectly. (Then threw them all away, because there's a reason mince pies are now vegetarian.)

I've made Christmassy pie charts and PowerPoints, line graphs and crosswords.

I've even had a couple of epic festive-themed fights with my parents, because laughing at a letter I wrote to Father Christmas when I was five years old is just *not* entering into the appropriate spirit of things.

And – most importantly – I've decorated.

In fact, thanks to school having just broken up for the Christmas holidays, my house is starting to look like something Santa would visit incognito out of sheer embarrassment.

I have Christmasified *everything*.

With barely contained happiness, I have glitterised and spangalised, frostificated and shimmerised. I have sparklificated and made up a whole range of festive verbs and written them in my notepad.

But it doesn't make much of a difference.

Because four days ago, in a dark TV studio in the middle of London, a beautiful model boy held my hand.

I had my First Ever Kiss.

And now it doesn't matter how much sparkle I spray, or glitter I drop: it feels like I'm decorating from the inside out.

The shiniest thing here this Christmas is *me*.

2

Here are some other important festive Firsts:

- The First Ever Christmas stamp was issued in 1962 and featured a wreath and two candles.
- The First Ever Christmas card was sold in 1843 and depicted a family drinking wine.
- The First Ever Christmas song sung in space was Jingle Bells.

Not that I'm trying to compare one kiss with significant festive moments that changed the entire course of human history.

But I think I know how their inventors felt.

It may have changed the course of mine.

"*And,*" I tell Nat, happily bouncing up and down on the sofa with a tiny red frosted T-rex on a string clutched between my hands, "we spend an average of *two weeks* of our lives just kissing. Isn't that *wonderful*?"

"Mmm," my best friend says, taking the dinosaur off me, frowning at it and putting it back in the decoration box.

"Plus each kiss burns up to three calories," I inform her, handing her a giraffe coated in green glitter. "That means it is *twice* as productive as sleeping."

"Wow," Nat says, putting that away too.

"And studies have shown that we remember *ninety per cent* of the details of our first kiss." I bounce up and down a few more times with a tin-foil robot. "Although in my case, I think it might be even more."

Like, ninety-nine per cent at the very least.

I remember *everything.*

I remember the quietness after everyone abruptly left us alone in the television studio, and the unexpected flush in Nick's cheeks when he told me he liked me.

I remember the way he reminded me all over again of a lion: big, wild hair and cat-shaped eyes and a mouth that curved upwards at the corners.

I remember the deep breath he took as he stepped forward.

The way he looked at every part of my face.

The way I studied every inch of his.

I can still see the ski-slope shape of his nose; smell the faint lime-green scent of his breath; feel the tickle of a dark curl against my forehead and how his bottom lip was warm and dry.

I can still feel the throb in my ears, and the heat in my cheeks, and the way my heart skittered around my chest like a deer on ice.

Literally still feel it.

Maybe I should work on not remembering quite so much. Kissing causes a sudden surge of dopamine and adrenaline through the system, and mine appears to have lasted three and a half whole days.

"Gosh," Nat says, handing me a boring gold bell and pointing firmly at the tree. "That. Is. Amazing."

"I *know.*" I beam at my best friend. Nat's been camped out at my house pretty much constantly since The Kiss happened. She claims it's to help me decorate, but I think I know the truth.

It's so I Don't Do Anything Stupid.

Which is totally unnecessary. I don't even know what that would be.

"*And,*" I continue breathlessly, gazing in rapture up at the beautiful, sparkling Christmas tree, "scientists say that five out of twelve cranial nerves in the brain light up when you kiss someone. You are *literally* connecting with your *minds*. Isn't that just the most romantic thing you've ever h—"

"OK," Nat says calmly, throwing a piece of red tinsel on the floor. "Enough."

I stare at it in consternation, and then at her.

"What are you talking about? You can *never* have enough tinsel, Natalie. *Never*. It is a *physical impossibility*."

Like time travel, or the ability to put a chocolate bar back in the fridge once the wrapper's open.

"No, I mean enough of *this*." Nat points at me. "Enough about kissing. Enough about Nick. Enough hopping up and down while I do all the decorating. It's time to stop now."

Huh. OK.

My adrenaline and dopamine levels are so high they've actually managed to seep out and exhaust my best friend too.

"I'm sorry," I say, obediently hanging a silver bauble on a lower branch. Nat's right: while I've been bouncing, she's decorated pretty much the whole tree. "It's just... It's all so *perfect*, Nat. Christmas, romance, my momentous coming of age as a kissable human being." I shake my head in wonder. "It really *is* the most magical time of the year."

There's a long silence.

The kind of silence you could wind round a fir tree, should you be interested in decorating with silences.

Then Nat sits down next to me and puts her

arm round my shoulder. "That's not what I meant," she says gently. "I meant... time's up."

Because the *main* reason my best friend hasn't left my side is it's been nearly four whole days now since I had my first kiss.

And Nick still hasn't called.

3

Obviously, I like rules.

Rules stop people cheating in exams, and filling out official documentation in pencil, or just putting the king anywhere they like in a game of chess. Rules prevent running in school corridors and walking all over the grass at Cambridge University like total savages.

Rules allow geeks like me to know what to

do, and when to do it, and then to try and make other people do it too, even when they don't really want to.

Rules put the world in order.

But as much as I like a good distinct rule, some are obviously more flexible and open to interpretation. More like – let's be honest – suggestions.

And I think the Three Day Rule is a *guideline*.

"But he's only six hours over the limit," I remind her. "It's been less than seventy-seven hours and fifty-three minutes since it happened."

I should know: I've programmed it into my stopwatch.

"Harriet," Nat sighs patiently, "if a boy doesn't make contact within three days, they're not going to. That's the *law*."

I frown. "Chickens aren't allowed to cross the road in Georgia: *that's* a law. Not having a sleeping donkey in your bathtub after 7pm in Oklahoma: *that's* a law. Using a phone is not actually a legal requirement."

Although frankly, of the three options, it's the one I'd vote for.

"Not a *law* law," my best friend admits reluctantly. "But it's the law of dating and everybody knows it."

"*I* didn't know it."

She nods as if this goes without saying. "Everybody *apart* from you. And maybe some random Inuit girl who's been buried under a pile of ice for the last twenty billion years and is still waiting for some idiot to ring her."

I laugh. "In fairness, the big bang only happened fourteen billion years ago, so the universe not existing yet is probably a legitimate excuse."

"It's the *only* legitimate excuse," she growls.

"And maybe Nick doesn't know the rules either," I add, ignoring her. "Statistically, the average phone is broken within eleven weeks. There are *many* possible reasons why he's not calling."

"Sure," Nat says darkly. "Maybe his fingers have been snapped off and fed to a party of hungry Christmas elves."

I laugh. I love my best friend when she gets

angry and protective. She starts staring into space and muttering threats like Batman.

But it's just not going to work.

Nat can be as cynical as she likes – there are *way* too many love chemicals currently rushing through my body for me to feel anxious. I am bouncing on a fluffy Christmas marshmallow of my own biological optimism.

It's kind of funny, really.

We both knew that eventually a boy would enter the equation for one of us first. It's just that in ten years of friendship, we never guessed that he might be for *me.*

"Have a little faith in romance," I say reassuringly, jumping up and skipping to the switch in the wall. "Trust in the magic of the season, Nat. Nothing's going to go wrong. It's *Christmas*."

Grinning, I switch the tree lights on with a tiny *pop*.

And – with a burst of 'Joy to the World' – my phone starts ringing.

4

Seriously.

My precognitive skills are totally wasted as a budding model. With my startling ability to see the future, I should at least be employed as some kind of psychic.

Although statistically most give forty-eight-hours' warning before something happens, so I'd definitely be one of the cheap ones.

Sticking my tongue out at Nat, I grab my

phone from where it's been perched on the arm of the sofa. It's a mysterious unrecognised number, and I'm so shiny now it's hard to tell which is more twinkly: me or the T-rex.

"Nick?" I beam into my phone.

"Sadly not, my little Elf. Although you can bet your sparkle-chickens I'm working on it. I keep trying to curl my hair like his, and then I am forced to remember I don't really have any."

Nat's making a frantic *who-is-it?* face, so I mouth back *Wilbur* and try not to notice the *I-told-you-so* eye-roll. For a few seconds I can feel my supreme confidence wobble slightly.

Four days *is* quite a long time.

I could have done half of the Trans-Siberian

Railway in the time it's taken the first recipient of my lips not to contact me.

"Wilbur, have you got a new number?"

"No, this phone belongs to the agency, Baby-cinnamon-socks. I dropped mine down the toilet. Nearly went from being my number one form of communication to my number two, if you know what I mean."

Then my modelling agent breaks into peals of tiny bell-like giggles.

"*Any*who," he continues, "I'm just calling to see if you got the new fashion contract from Yuka Ito before the Christmas holidays start. That is *not* a designer who waits, even for little baby Jesus."

"Sure," I say, making a *cut-it-out* face at Nat. She's formed a gun with her hands and is pointing it angrily at a tiny cupid hanging on the tree. "My parents signed it, it's all fine and it's in the p—"

I stop abruptly.

Ooh. I've just had a brilliant idea. A brilliant, inspired, really quite obvious idea I'd have had ages ago if I wasn't so busy having a happy festive meltdown.

And also writing hilarious legal Clauses for Santa.

"Wilbur, do you have Nick's phone number? Could you maybe give it to me?"

Nat stops shooting Cupid and her eyes go very round. In fairness, this is definitely, *definitely* not in the dating rules. She's told me so about a billion times, vehemently.

The girl must never contact the boy first. Ever.

Especially if he disappeared so quickly he didn't actually give her his number, so she couldn't call him in the first place.

"They're *not rules*," I hiss at Nat for the trillionth time, holding my hand over the phone. "They're *guidelines*."

"Darling," Wilbur laughs, "if I gave Nick's number to every girl who rang asking for Nick's number, I'd basically be a telephone directory. Also, as he's one of our models, it's data protected."

"Oh." I can feel myself collapse slightly again. "Of course. Sorry. Well, Merry Christm—"

"But as it's you... I heard the most *amusalazing* story the other day. Do you want to hear it? Do you have a piece of paper and a pen handy?"

I blink a few times.

"Umm," I say vaguely, watching Nat pick up a sugar mouse and then pointedly bite its head off. "Sure?"

"Ready?" He clears his throat ostentatiously. "*Oh*, my dear, once upon a time *seven* little boys made *seven* little snowmen and *oh* can you believe each hand had *nine* fingers so—"

"What were they made of?"

"Sorry, Bunny?"

"What were the snowmen's fingers made of? Because it can't be snow – I've tried that and they don't stay on. And you can make *arms* out of sticks or brooms, but *fingers* are really tricky."

There's a pause, and then a long sigh.

"I don't think you quite understand the point

of this story, Twinkle-face. Maybe I'll try a simpler one." Wilbur clears his throat. "*Oh* every Christmas time *seven* elves prepare *seven* stockings but *oh zero* of them have time to wrap more than *nine* gifts—"

"*Seven* elves?" I interrupt again. "There are approximately two billion children in the world, Wilbur. Even with nine gifts each that wouldn't be enough to—"

"*Oh* for the love of brandy pudding," Wilbur exhales. "Do you want this story, poppet, or do you want to spend Christmas cuddling your oversized teddy bear instead?"

I blink. How does he know about my teddy b—

Hang on. *Oh*. Seven elves. Seven snowmen. *Oh seven seven.*

A wave of disbelief smashes over my head.

Oh my God. Wilbur's telling me Nick's mobile phone number and I'm too busy correcting him to actually notice. My love life is about to go down the pan thanks to my chronic pedantry.

I am such an accurate *idiot.*

Fast as I can, I rip the back off a Christmas card. It's from Granny Manners and it has red bows stuck all over the front of it. In fairness, it probably needed destroying eventually anyway.

"Shoot," I say, grabbing one of Nat's eyeliners. "There were nine gifts, how many fingers? Or was it stockings?"

"I'm texting it to you now," Wilbur says in defeat. "Don't say it came from me."

A rush of gratitude whooshes over me.

"*Thank you thank you,* Wilbur. You're the best."

"You bet your tiny jingle-bells I am," he laughs. "Merry Christmas, my little Snow-socks. Now go get him."

5

Which is exactly what I intend to do.

There's just one hurdle standing between my romantic Christmas destiny and me. And she's looming directly over me with her hands on her hips and the string tail of a mouse dangling out of her mouth.

It's really quite distracting.

Nat looks exactly like our cat Victor after he's been on a successful hunt in the garden.

Except high on sugar and pink food colouring, and therefore a lot more dangerous.

"*This*," my best friend says crossly, taking a step towards me, "is exactly why I've been stuck to you for four days, Harriet Manners."

Ha. Told you that's why she's really here.

"Natalie," I say quickly, holding my phone over my head as the text received sound pings. "Did Jane Bennet just sit around, waiting for Bingley to call her? *No.* She went to his house, uninvited, and pretended it was to see his sisters and got the flu and stayed there for *weeks*, remember?"

Nat frowns. "*That's* the example you're using? Seriously?"

I clear my throat: OK, point made.

"How about Lizzy Bennet?" I say, quickly

tapping open my messages. "Did she just sit around, waiting for Darcy to make the move?"

"Nope," Nat says, taking another step. "She got on with her own life and started making out with Wickham instead."

Sugar cookies. Thanks to a plethora of well-made and accurate Hollywood adaptations, she's right again.

"Cinderella?" I say desperately, stabbing at the number Wilbur has sent me. "She went to the ball without being invited, right? Breaking the rules worked for her just fine."

"Harriet," Nat says, holding her hands out. "Firstly, Cinderella's the least cool fairy-tale heroine ever invented. Secondly, you are *not* a rule breaker. And thirdly, do you really *want* to talk to someone who doesn't want to talk to you?"

I stare at her in amazement.

Of course I do. I want to talk to people who don't want to talk to me all the time.

My best friend clearly doesn't know me *at all*.

Besides…

"But you're wrong," I say in confusion. "He's been waiting for the right moment. And that moment is right now. Just watch."

With a final burst of confidence, I hit call number and beam smugly at Nat as it rings twice.

There's a tiny click.

"Hello?" a familiar, warm, twangy Australian voice says. "Nick speaking."

And it's like magic.

With just three words, every gorgeous romantic moment from the last couple of weeks comes racing straight back.

"Hey, Nick," I say brightly as something in the middle of me starts spinning happily like a Christmas bauble, glittering all over. "It's me."

Then there's a pause long enough for me to fully register the significance of what I've just done.

"Sorry," Lion Boy says eventually, "who?"

6

There are 1,025,109.8 known words currently in the English language.

'*Who*' was the only one I wasn't prepared for.

I put my name and number into Nick's phone myself, with my own fingers. Which means that he didn't just fail to use my details in the last four days...

He actually *deleted* them?

45

"It's Harriet," I say stupidly as Nat puts her hands over her mouth in horror. "Harriet Manners."

Norwegian scientists have hypothesised that Rudolph's red nose is probably the result of a parasitic infection of the respiratory system.

Judging by my current glow and sudden inability to breathe, I should be able to lead Santa through the night quite safely for some years to come.

"We kissed a few days ago," I clarify into the aching silence, and then add in a panic: "Speaking of kissing, did you know that the word mistletoe comes from the Old English word *mistletan,* which means *poo twig,* because it spreads itself through seeds in bird droppings that land on tree branches?"

Nat's eyes are now so round they look like they're about to pop out and roll under a table.

Poo twig? she mouths at me.

"*And*," I continue with a wince, turning round to rest my hot forehead on the wall, "don't you think it's strange that an entire romantic tradition is based around a parasitic plant that takes nutrients from another? What does that say about love, do you think?"

Oh my God. I can't stop talking.

I'm going to just keep talking, and when the heat from my cheeks causes the whole house to explode into flames and crumble around me, I'll be there: still inexplicably yabbering about parasites.

Frankly, I've read a lot of romantic speeches

in my life, and absolutely *none* of them started with faeces.

"Although," I add in a desperate, horrified rush, "apparently mistletoe actually comes from a Norse legend and the white berries are—"

"Stop, Harriet," Nick laughs. "I believe it's you. No further evidence is necessary. Where on earth are you calling from?"

"England. My living room."

I'm pretty much part of the wall now, but he doesn't need to know that.

"Very literal." He laughs again. There's a crispy chomping sound. "I'm in the kitchen, eating cereal for lunch because apparently I don't know how to fend for myself." There's the crunchy sound of a cornflake box being shaken. "So... is there a problem?"

I blink, smacking my head gently on the wall. "Umm, sorry?"

"You called me." A second shake. "Is something wrong?"

Oh my God. This is getting worse by the minute. Apparently my call is *so* unwelcome and *so* unexpected it's actually a sign that the universe has gone awry.

"No-o-o. I just…" I clear my throat. "I wanted to say hello, that's all. Thomas Edison chose it as the word to use when greeting people on the phone. So… hello."

I can hear Nat make a tiny humiliated squeak behind me. Nothing says *romance* like poo and the man who invented the nickel-iron battery.

"Hello to you too." There's a third cornflake shake, and even through my waves of shame

I can't help being surprised: exactly how much fibre does this boy *need*? "So are you excited about this afternoon?"

This conversation is getting weirder and weirder. Am I excited about this afternoon?

Obviously I am.

It's six days before Christmas. Traditionally, Nat and I spend the afternoon after we decorate the tree trying to make my dog wear a Santa outfit and attempting to encourage my dad not to.

"Ye-e-es?" I say slowly. "You?"

"Definitely." A fourth shake of cornflakes. "I can't think of a more perfect time of year for a date."

7

Here's the final fact I know about Rudolph:

Never mind that she's actually female; forget the probability that she's very sick with a potentially dangerous respiratory infection.

Science has calculated that if she ever actually managed to get up in the air, the speed required to fly around the world on Christmas Day would mean that she'd vaporise within 4.26 seconds flat.

I can really empathise.

Five minutes ago, I was as high up as it was possible to get; now I'm plummeting to the ground in a big humiliated ball of flames.

Nick is going on a *date*?

Oh my God, no wonder he's been so quiet: he deleted my number, forgot I existed and started arranging an epic festive romance with somebody *else*.

This is why I should always follow rules.

"D-date?" I finally manage. "Like, a *courtship* date? Or a… dried oblong fleshy fruit which is originally from northern Africa?"

I don't know why I said that. He obviously didn't mean winter was a nice time to eat the fruit of a *Phoenix dactylifera*.

There's a loud laugh.

"*Courtship*. That's a word I don't hear much. Yes, I guess I mean a throw-pebbles-at-a-window, sing-by-the-light-of-the-moon, black-and-white-movie kind of date. Is that OK with you?"

Right, I take it back. This isn't the most magical season at all.

Christmas officially *sucks*.

Quickly, claw back some dignity, Harriet.

"Of course it's OK," I say sharply. "My big date *tomorrow* is going to be *super* romantic. There will probably be... candles. And flowers. And... umm... flowery candles. And candles with flowers on them. And in them."

I have clearly never been out with a boy in my entire life.

Or seen a candle, quite possibly.

"You have a date tomorrow?"

He doesn't need to sound so surprised. "Of course I do, Nicholas. It's *Christmas*. The season of *romance*. His name is..." I look desperately round the room. My dog, Hugo, is sitting quietly in the corner under the tree, chewing on the fairy that's supposed to go on top of it. Victor the cat is watching him with undiluted disgust. "His name is... Umm... Hugo. Victor Hugo."

Nat gives another horrified squeak.

"Except not the one who wrote *Les Miserables*," I clarify quickly. "A totally different and less dead one."

"Right." Nick clears his throat. "Well, that's... cool. If you want to postpone or cancel this afternoon, just let me know."

And a surge of fizzling anger suddenly whips through me.

You know what? This is *so* typical.

First a boy kisses you at Christmas time. Then he doesn't contact you for four days. Then you ring *him*, and he tells you he's going on a date. And then he has the *audacity* to try and alter your plans for the afternoon when you've already—

Hang on.

"Cancel this afternoon? Nick, what the… how the… what the sugar cookies are you talking about?"

"Our date. Me. You. Remember?" There's another pause. "Jeez, Harriet, I'm not feeling great about my kissing skills right now."

What?

As fast as I can, I rack my brain for *any* conversation I might have inadvertently had with Nick over the last four days. Am I *so* good at dating I've managed to arrange one without actually being aware of it?

"But... we haven't spoken since I last saw you."

"Well *no*," he says slowly. "Because you said you hate talking on the phone. But we've *messaged* a lot, and planned the whole thing out, and... you... said..."

He slows to a stop.

"I said what?" I'm genuinely curious. "What did I say?"

"You wrote ROFFL a lot," he finishes flatly. "With two Fs. And LOLZ. And you spelt *later* with an eight and *see you* as C and U. Oh my

God. You were called Hunnygurl and your profile pic was a pair of pink high heels. Who the *hell* have I been talking to?"

And – as if a choir of angels has burst into sudden song – everything abruptly slots into place.

My hands must have been *so* sweaty and excited after my first ever kiss, they managed to slip and put a complete stranger's number into his phone. Because that is exactly the kind of idiotic thing I would do.

Obviously supermodel Nick has an amazing profile photo: I don't even blame them for giving it a shot.

The biggest Christmas tree in the world is in Rio de Janeiro. It is 278 feet tall, and floats on the Rodrigo de Freitas Lagoon.

As I turn slowly to face Nat again, I think I could now give that tree a run for its money.

I am considerably shinier and floatier.

"So I'm seeing you this afternoon?" I clarify as Nat starts jumping up and down as silently as possible with her hands in the air.

"Hopefully," Nick laughs. "And possibly a third, unknown, person with painful feet and a tendency to abbreviate. You in?"

Nat and I give each other the quietest high-five ever achieved in the history of high-fives, and then she starts dancing around the living room.

I turn back to the phone with all 3.3 million of my internal fairy lights burning.

"Definitely. It's a date."

8

Here are a few examples of how Christmas is celebrated around the world:

- In the Ukraine, Christmas trees are decorated with spider's webs.
- In Scandinavia, they leave porridge out for Santa instead of cookies.
- In Greenland, they eat Kiviak, a decomposed bird wrapped in seal-skin and buried under rocks for many months.

- *In Italy, presents are delivered on a broomstick.*
- *In Serbia, children tie their fathers up on the Sunday before Christmas until they get their gifts.*

I think that last one is an excellent idea.

In fact, on days like this I think maybe we should introduce it.

And I'd happily forgo the presents.

"Harriet," my father says as I race with Nat up the stairs as fast as our legs will carry us, "why did Santa's helper go to see the doctor?"

Without a word, Nat opens my wardrobe and starts pulling out clothes in a panic.

"Why, Dad?" I say distractedly as he follows us into my room. Nat holds up a reindeer jumper and then inexplicably makes a sick face and throws it on the floor.

"Because he had low *elf-esteem*." Dad crinkles up with laughter. "And, Harriet?"

Nat drops to the ground like a soldier and starts rummaging round on the floor through my selection of trainers and flip-flops.

"What, Dad?"

"Harriet, how do snowmen get around?"

I'm urgently tugging out of a drawer every single pair of trousers I own: jeans, culottes, shorts, leggings. The bottom half of a furry koala-bear outfit I made in Year Eight that still rather worryingly fits.

"I don't know," I say as Nat pointedly puts the koala back in the wardrobe.

"By *icicle*," Dad declares, chortling even

harder. "And, Harriet, why does Santa have three—"

"*Dad.*" Seriously. From the moment December hits, my father turns into a one-man cracker joke. It's like the worst metamorphosis in the history of transformations. "I'm kind of busy right now."

According to the new countdown on my stopwatch, I have fifty-three minutes before I have to leave for my First Ever Date.

As befits school holidays, I haven't taken my penguin pyjamas off for days, I'm covered in dog hair from all the extra Hugo cuddle-time and there are mince-pie crumbs in my hair.

Plus, I realise as I glance quickly in the mirror, I still have icing sugar in my eyebrows from the biscuits I made yesterday.

You can talk about my natural elegance as much as you like – although nobody ever does – but I'm slowly turning into one of The Twits. I clearly have a lot of work to do.

And *fast.*

"But, Harriet," Dad says, head still poking through my bedroom doorway, "I really need to know what Santa's favourite pizza is. Do you think it's deep and crisp and ev—"

"What's happening?" Annabel says as I finish Dad's sentence by putting my hand on his chest and physically pushing him out of the room. "Richard, that book of jokes is going in the bin. You're ruining Christmas for everyone."

Then my stepmother leans curiously in through the doorway. Her little round pregnant belly is definitely protruding now. We've had a lot of festive fun, making her laugh and then comparing it to a bowl full of jelly.

She's taken it very well, considering.

"Harriet," she says calmly, resting her head on the doorframe, "why are you dismantling your bedroom? And hello, Natalie. You did a great job with the tree – it looks very traditional. There's a distinct lack of handmade cardboard hippos, so I suspect you did the majority."

"Thanks, Annabel." Nat pauses rummaging to study a piece of paper. "I'd give you a hug, but we've got *so much to do.*"

Frankly, I don't have time to worry about this slight to my decorating skills. After Nick and I said goodbye, Nat and I hopped straight on the internet and Googled *How do you date?*

My best friend may be the coolest person I

know, but this is uncharted territory for both of us: we might as well have landed on Pluto.

If Pluto was a planet with apparently rigid rules about what shade of lipstick to wear so you don't look too available, obviously.

Apparently it's a very long list.

"Do for what?" Annabel says, frowning. "Where are you two going in such a hurry?"

"Well," I say, glancing pointedly at my best friend. At pivotal times like this, it's lucky we work so perfectly together. Like holly and ivy, or brandy and butter, or Brussels sprouts and the bin. "We just thought we'd go to the cinem—"

"Harriet has a *date*!" Nat yells jubilantly, throwing my purple sock in the air like some kind of celebratory firecracker. "A real date!

With a real boy! A living one! One that breathes! This afternoon! In London! Whoop whoop!"

Then she triumphantly holds her hand up to high-five me again. I shake my head at it sadly.

Because as my lovely but super-strict stepmother frowns and grabs the list out of my best friend's overexcited grip, I'm not sure there's much point in getting dressed after all.

I'm not going anywhere.

9

OK, Nat and I may need to work on our telepathy skills. That mind-reading board game I forced her to play all summer clearly didn't work.

Annabel looks at the list we wrote.

She looks at us both, sitting on the floor surrounded by an emergency explosion of almost every possession I own (I dragged a few history and geography books down as well, just for good measure).

Then she hands the list to my father. "What do you make of this?"

Dad stares at the piece of paper with his forehead furrowed. He has sugar in his eyebrows too, and he didn't even make the biscuits.

How to Ace a Date!

- Pick an attractive outfit in advance and get plenty of beauty sleep!
- Google him before you go! ✔
- Charm him with information about himself and use his full name to create an air of intimacy!
- Laugh at all his jokes and find an excuse to subtly touch him!

- Compliment him – find something you have in common!
- Steal his heart with a two-second glance away (diagram attached)!
- Have a long, luxurious bath before you go!

I think it goes without saying I ticked one of those off some time ago. The rest were going to be a challenge, given that this is me we're talking about, but I was prepared to give it my very best shot.

"Where did you get this from?" Dad says, looking back at us. "Annabel, what kind of books do we keep in this house?"

My stepmother raises her eyebrows. "Oh, that must be an extract from the 1950s manual I follow on How To Be A Good Woman."

They stare at each other for a few seconds.

Then they both crease up in hysterical laughter and do a little fist bump.

"*Excuse me*," I say indignantly, standing up and putting my hands on my hips, "this is a *legitimate* and *accurate* list we have selected, edited and compiled from various *women's sites* on the *internet*. You are just too *old* to understand how *modern dating* works."

"This is probably true," Annabel agrees, nostrils still flaring. "When *we* dated, the excitement mainly came from running away from all the dinosaurs."

"That brontosaurus was such a pain, wasn't he?" Dad sighs, shaking his head. "Always getting in front of us with his big old spikes while we were trying to watch a film."

"Couldn't eat a romantic spaghetti dinner without a pterodactyl swooping down to take a meatball."

"And just *try* climbing a balcony to serenade without a diplodocus licking your ear."

"Times have indeed changed."

I stare at both of them. I know enough about the timeline of earth's history to realise they're joking, but I'm pretty sure humour's supposed to be funny.

One day somebody needs to tell them that.

"Firstly," I say indignantly, "brontosauruses didn't *have* spikes. You're thinking of a stegosaurus. Secondly, pterodactyls were *not* actually dinosaurs. And thirdly, you're lucky you found each other because frankly I'm not sure anyone else would take you."

"That's kind of the point, isn't it?" Annabel laughs as Dad flies around the room, making a noise that presumably is supposed to resemble the prehistoric ancestor of the chicken.

Then she scrunches the list into a tight paper ball.

Nat and I look at each other in horror.

"Harriet," Annabel says firmly. "It is *not* your job to wear the right thing, or say the right thing, or do the right thing to make a boy like you. It is not your job to be pretty or make a boy feel good about himself."

She throws the paper into the bin.

"It *is* your job," she continues, "to be yourself, and if he likes that then *maybe* – just maybe, if you decide you like him too – he can stick around. Am I making myself perfectly, abundantly and permanently clear?"

Nat is staring at Annabel as if she's shining with a bright white, omniscient light, and I can kind of see why. It's a bit like having Merlin for a stepmother.

If Merlin was wearing a pinstripe suit with white fluffy snowman slippers.

"Yes," I say in awe. "Super clear."

"You were so worth fighting a triceratops for," Dad says proudly, putting his arm round her. Then he wrinkles his nose at me. "Although the bath advice was valid. Harriet, I love you, but when was the last time you showered?"

I glance down. There's an oat stuck to one of the penguins on my PJs.

Then I glance back up in surprise.

"Wait…" Something else has just clicked. "Does that mean…? Are you saying I can *go*?"

Annabel and Dad glance at each other.

"What do you think?"

"I think it's Christmas," Dad says thoughtfully. "I think it's the season of romance. I think Nick's *very* dashing and if we try to stop her she's going to climb out of her bedroom window."

I can feel myself flushing bright red.

I may not be the most athletic girl in the world, but for once they might have a point: I am quite obviously *very* keen.

They just don't need to point it out *in front of me.*

"Fine," Annabel nods. "You'll have your phone on you at all times. You'll text when you arrive safely and when you're about to leave, and you'll be home by eight on the dot or there will be a world of trouble. Deal?"

I nearly crush both her and my unborn sibling with the force of my grateful hug.

I really *love* this time of year.

"Deal."

10

Apparently, the destination of my first ever date is supposed to be a big and super-romantic surprise.

Nick was *very* specific about that.

"I'm not telling you where we're going, Harriet," he said when I tried to find out more. "Just remember to bring gloves, OK?"

"OK," I agreed, and didn't ask any more insightful questions. Mainly because I didn't need to: we're going to the Science Museum.

How do I know this?

Because we're meeting at the underground exit of South Kensington tube station in London, and I've been travelling to and from there with my dad for the last ten years. When I was eight, I sent the museum so many challenging letters about steam engines they offered me a lifetime membership just to reward my enthusiasm.

And also possibly to save on postage.

Plus the gloves are a total giveaway. Over eighty per cent of infectious diseases are transmitted through touch, and interactive exhibitions are extremely popular with small children. I have a stretchy blue rubber pair I borrowed from the Science department at school especially.

And I don't enjoy surprises.

Nick clearly still has a *lot* to learn about me.

Knowing precisely what the romantic plans are, however, hasn't helped my nerves. By the time I've walked to the train station, I'm shaking so hard I'm basically vibrating.

On the upside, at least it's warmed me up.

I'm in cosy winter clothes, but at 3:30pm it's already starting to get dark, and it's absolutely freezing. After much deliberation, Nat and I settled on my favourite big Christmas jumper (red with an enormous green sequined holly stitched to the front), thick black leggings lined with fluff, boots, red socks and a red woolly bobble hat and mittens.

"Hey," my best friend pointed out

sympathetically when I tugged my red hooded duffle coat on over the top, "if Nick *wanted* glamour, he'd probably have asked out somebody else, right?"

I'm pretty sure she meant it in a nice way.

The only problem now is that – thanks to a combination of cold, nerves, excitement, clothes, hair and the unexpected warmth of the London Underground – I'm essentially scarlet all over.

And as I start jittering in terror off the Underground train on to the platform of South Kensington station, I think I might be slowly turning green as well. Scholars at Cambridge University believe the traditional Christmas colours of green and red originated from Celt stories told many centuries ago.

Theologians disagree.

Either way, thanks to overheating and nearly vomiting on the escalators, I'm about as festive as a human gets.

Still shaking, I emerge anxiously from the tube gates a full fifteen minutes early, turn right and start the familiar long walk down the underground tunnel towards the museum exits.

I know every tiny detail of this journey.

I know the exposed, grey-yellow brickwork and the bright butterfly posters and the curving overhead arches. I'm familiar with the sharp swerves of the cement path and the line of bright lights running down the middle.

I know it was built in 1883 after the success

of a Fisheries exhibition and a toll of one old penny was charged to walk down it.

None of which is the slightest use to me right now.

All I can see is Nick.

As I walk slowly forward, I see the first time I met him by crawling under a table at the Clothes Show Live, and how my first ever words to him were about the illegality of chewing gum in Singapore.

I see the afternoon I sat on the pavement outside the modelling agency, hyperventilating into my hands.

I see when I asked him to sniff them.

I see rolling on to the fashion shoot in Red Square in a wheelchair and starting a fight with him about Pooh Bear on national television.

I see our phone conversation three hours ago.

In short, the closer I get to Nick, the harder it hits me just how much of an idiot I always am in front of him, every single time.

Literally. Without exception.

Despite how statistically unlikely that is, or the fact that you'd think I'd learn from at least *some* of my mistakes.

And with every step my idiocy just keeps hitting me over and over again, until it takes every bit of courage I have not to pull my red bobble hat over my face and run back to the safety of a family-sized tin of chocolates I have absolutely no intention of sharing with my family.

Instead, I take the deepest breath I can find.

I blow it out shakily and watch it hang in the cold air in front of me.

I remind myself that we've already kissed, so the chances of him screaming out loud in horror when he sees me must be at least *slightly* reduced.

Then I stand in front of a busker with my sweaty hands clenched tightly into fists inside my mittens. The busker's sitting on the floor of the tunnel surrounded by a large crowd, blowing 'White Christmas' into an orange traffic cone as if it's a trumpet, and it's surprisingly calming.

All I need is a little time to collect my thoughts.

Just a few extra moments to dry my palms, adjust my breathing and maybe check the internet for *How To Run Away From A Date At The Last Minute*.

But the problem is: I can still see Nick.

I can still see big, unruly black curls and almond-shaped eyes, brown skin and a mole on the upper left cheekbone. I can still see a ski-slope nose and pointed leonine teeth, and a too-wide mouth that breaks his face in half when he smiles.

And as a tall boy wearing a big grey army coat at the front of the crowd turns and grins straight at me, I now mean that literally.

Nick holds his hand up and smiles a bit harder.

My head immediately empties.

I guess I'm not collecting any thoughts today after all.

||

Slowly, Lion Boy makes his way through the crowd towards me.

He's grinning so hard now his eyes are crinkled up and glowing. Which is somewhat fitting, because something very similar is now happening to the contents of my ribcage.

"Hey," he says as soon as he can be heard over the trumpeting busker, smiling even wider. "Great minds."

90

My hands are sweating, my stomach is spinning a bit like a roasting pig's head, and I can feel overwhelming panic starting to climb up my throat. I'd forgotten quite how beautiful this boy is, and exactly what he does to my heartbeat.

Last time Nick and I were together, we were kissing.

So what happens now? Do we kiss again straight away? Fist-bump? Hug? Bow? Stick our tongues out at each other like they do in Tibet or sniff each other like on the Polynesian island of Tuvalu?

He leans forward to kiss my cheek at the exact moment I go to politely shake his hand, which means I accidentally stab him hard in the stomach with my fingers.

Nice one, Harriet. The Heimlich manoeuvre. A traditional romantic greeting.

"Mmmm," I mumble nervously. "I've really only considered traffic cones useful for redirecting cars."

Nick looks confused, then glances behind him and laughs. "I meant us both getting here early. But you're right, the busker's a genius. Apparently he calls himself *Big Jam*."

I nod nervously. "C-cool. I really like jam too. Strawberry's my favourite, although in the United States it's second in popularity to grape but one place above raspberry."

Then I blink. Where did *that* come from?

Nowhere at any point did a woman's magazine suggest opening with statistics about American preserves.

"I assumed it was a pun," Nick laughs again. "Traffic jam, music jam?"

Sugar cookies. Obviously it is.

I'm just way too anxious to appreciate cunning roadwork wordplay right now. Instead I clear my throat and stare awkwardly at the floor while my brain scrambles around in a panic for something to save it.

Quickly, Harriet. You're failing already.

Forget Annabel: this is no time to start free styling. Revert to Plan A before you ruin everything.

Trembling, I take a deep breath, mentally grab the list out of the bin and desperately try to remember what I can. Then I obediently throw my head back and giggle as ferociously as I can.

"Jam!" I exclaim as loudly as possible,

fluttering my eyelashes so quickly my eyes start to water. "Goodness me, Nicholas Hidaka, you are *uproarious.*"

Then I mentally tick a few points off.

1. *Laugh at all his jokes* ✓
2. *Use his full name* ✓
3. *Find an excuse to touch him* ✓

Luckily I got the last point out of the way a few minutes ago, thanks to trying to dislodge his stomach with my fingers.

"Umm." Nick blinks. "It's not my joke, but thank you?"

"You're welcome," I say stiffly, then swallow hard. "Also... I'd like you to know that I find your bicep muscles very..." *Striated with*

myofilaments? Attached to bone with tendons?
Biologically necessary for arm movement?
"Bicep-y."

Nick's eyebrows shoot upwards. *Bicepy.* That would make a good name for a baby bison.

Then I quickly count *one elephant, two elephants,* look away, and glance back and upwards at approximately a thirty-degree angle.

4. *Compliment him* ✓
5. *Steal his heart with a two-second glance away* ✓

"...Thanks again," Nick says as we start walking down the familiar tunnel. "I was... umm... born with muscles in the top of my arms. Like most humans."

Thank goodness I'm already wearing red.

Nat and I found scientific evidence that wearing red makes people more attractive. OK, it said *little red dress* and all I had was a big red jumper and a bobble hat, but it's pretty much the same thing.

Combined with the colour of my cheeks, that's one less thing to worry about.

"And," I say, grabbing a strand of hair before realising it's not long enough to twiddle coyly, "you come from Australia and are 187.96 centimetres tall. Which do you think is better? Madrid Fashion Week or Paris Fashion Week?"

6. *Charm him with information about himself* ✓

7. *Find something you have in common* ✓

All I could think of was modelling.

Let's hope he takes the conversation over from here because that is the sum total of my entire fashion knowledge.

"Harriet," Nick frowns as we begin climbing the steps towards the Science Museum, "are you OK? You're being a bit..."

Attractive? Seductive? Irresistible in a powerful yet subtle and sophisticated way?

"...un-Harriet," he finishes.

Oh my God. I must have remembered the list wrong. Maybe it needs to be in the correct order to work.

"I'm fine!" I squeak. If in doubt, *always* turn to science. "In fact, have you noticed that my pupils are probably fully dilated? Also, I'm pretty sure my white-blood-cell count is really high too."

Both of which are indisputable biological signs that I'm flirting as hard as I possibly can.

We've reached the top of the exit stairs.

The air is so cold I can see both our breaths wafting like dragon puffs in front of us. I'm staring hard at the floor, and every part of my face and ears is starting to tingle and burn.

I don't think it's because of the weather.

Never mind a disaster: this is rapidly turning into the dating equivalent of the bubonic plague, which wiped out sixty per cent of Europe in the fourteenth century: i.e. one of the most destructive catastrophes the world has ever witnessed.

I've never seen the normally laid-back Nick look so confused before, or like maybe he wants to be somewhere else.

Like, literally anywhere.

"Harriet," Nick says slowly, frowning and bending down slightly so he can see my face. "What's going on? Don't you want to be here?"

"N-n-no," I stammer in horror. He thinks I'm sabotaging this date *on purpose?* "I mean y-yes. I mean of course I—"

Then I abruptly stop talking.

And it's not because I'm worried I'm about to say something else stupid, or do something even more ridiculous, or screw this situation up more horribly. It's not because I'm concerned I could take a magical romantic connection and destroy it even more thoroughly than I have already.

It's not *even* because I think this terrible, humiliating date could possibly go any worse.

Nope.

It's because I just heard a loud burst of 'Good King Wenceslas' playing fifteen feet to my right.

Which means it already has.

12

I don't believe it.

Which is kind of the problem.

I should have seen *this* dating disaster coming a mile off. Something is starting to tell me I may have been focusing on the wrong things.

"What's going on?" Nick says as I spin round just in time to see a blue trainer with a piano lace disappear behind a stone pillar. "Who's that?"

And I officially give up.

It was nice, having a love life for about three and a half minutes. I'm going to miss it.

"I'm sorry, Nick," I mumble, putting a hand briefly over my eyes. "For everything."

Then I take a deep breath, point in the opposite direction and say loudly: "Oh look. Was that a *Panthera pardus orientalis* wandering past?"

And out pops Toby.

You know the *Jaws* music that plays every time the shark gets close to its victim?

This Christmas, my stalker has his own version.

Except instead of *der-der, der-der, der-der*, he has a fluffy white jumper that plays 'Good King Wenceslas' really loudly.

I've been hearing it every time Toby accidentally makes an abrupt movement for the last three days.

"*Where*?" Toby says in excitement, spinning in tiny circles. "There are only twenty adult Amur leopards in existence, Harriet Manners. It's *very* unlikely one of them is roaming around Kensington, but *can you imagine*?"

His hair is flat to his head, his brown corduroys are covered in leaves and his nose is very wet looking. Whatever I did in a past life to deserve this final nail in the dating coffin, I'd like to apologise.

It must have been truly awful.

"*Toby,*" I hiss. "What are you *doing here*?"

"I'm just checking you're OK, Harriet," he says, wiping his nose on his jumper sleeve and leaving a long, glittering trail of snot. "I don't want you to end up romantically linked to a total weirdo."

Irony is going to make my head explode.

"Yes," I say sharply, unable to even look at my date any more, "like the kind of weirdo who would *stalk me all the way to London*."

"Exactly. You have to be super careful these days." Then Toby holds his hand out cheerfully to Nick. "Hello. I'm Toby Pilgrim, Harriet's stalker, friend and your new lifelong nemesis. I don't think we've been introduced yet."

'Good King Wenceslas' kicks in again.

I hadn't realised the jumper had flashing white lights in a Christmas tree shape as well.

Of course it does.

"Nick." I flush. "You don't have to—"

"Hi, Toby," Nick says warmly, shaking his hand. "Great to meet you. Have you been waiting for us long?"

"Only about half an hour. Natalie told me definitely *not* to follow Harriet on the 4:32 train to South Kensington via Kings Cross, so I knew to get the earlier one."

Nat. I cannot believe my best friend is using my stalker as her own personal spy.

"Great jumper, by the way," Nick grins, taking a step back so he can assess it. "My aunt bought me one that played 'Silent Night' but I've never had the guts to wear it."

I stare at him in surprise, but his expression is totally genuine. I'm guessing he doesn't mean Yuka.

"It *does* take a certain level of bravery and

style to work musical fashion," Toby agrees smugly. "I doubt you have it, Nicholas Hidaka. Also everybody knows 'Silent Night' is the least cool carol. You'd have looked absolutely ridiculous."

"*Toby*." I flush a bit harder as Nick laughs. "*Please stop.*"

Toby looks down sadly at his still-flashing stomach. "Technology has let me down yet again, Harriet."

Oh for the love of...

With a tiny sigh of resignation, I lean forward and click the *off* button so he at least stops pulsing for the next few minutes. "I'll try again," I say more gently. "Have you quite finished now, Toby?"

Then I give him a look that means in no

uncertain terms: *you have quite finished now, Toby.*

"Not quite," he replies chirpily. "But it shouldn't take too much longer." Then – with a series of soggy sniffles – he gets a notepad and pen out of his turtle-shaped satchel and turns to Nick.

Every year in the UK, approximately 1,300 home fires are caused by open candles, the majority of which happen in December. Honestly, I'm starting to realise that Christmas is actually an incredibly dangerous time of year.

I'm about to burst into flames as well.

"Ready?" Toby says, prodding Nick sharply with his pen. "I don't give half-marks or pity points, so you're going to have to *concentrate.*"

With a lurch of horror, I can just see *The*

Harriet Manners Quiz For Acceptable Suitors written at the top of the page in neat fountain pen. With a top hat drawn next to it.

And what appears to be a seal with a moustache.

Plus a blue spaceship.

No. This can't be happening No. No no no no nonononoNONONONO—

"Question one," Toby says with a broad smile. "Who was Gary Gygax?"

13

OK:

a) There's a Dating Harriet *quiz*?
b) Is it weird that I kind of want to take it myself?

"No no no," I squeak out loud, jumping forward and trying to rip it from Toby's grip. "Nick, you really don't have to—"

"Gary Gygax was the inventor of Dungeons & Dragons," my date says with a small smile. "Next?"

I pause with a stunned hand in the air.

Huh?

"Excellent," Toby says, making a little mark. "What word did Marvel Comics officially own between the years 1975 and 1996?"

Nick frowns. "*Zombie*. They also own *thwip*, which is the sound Spiderman's shooters make, and *snikt* from Wolverine's claws."

Then he gives me a little wry *what?* shrug.

"Comic fan," he explains modestly. "When I was ten I inherited about two hundred."

"Point," Toby says, making a little note. "Although you're not getting any extra marks. Next – Asterix versus Popeye in a fight?"

"Asterix pre-spinach, Popeye post-spinach."

Tick. "Would you ever wear white socks with black shoes?"

I can see the change of handwriting on the list. That one's definitely coming from Nat.

"Yes. If I can't find black ones, any socks will do."

This earns him a cross. "Hogwarts house?"

"Gryffindor." Nick grimaces, pulling a face at me as I let out a tiny Ravenclaw groan. "Sorry about that."

Sugar cookies. I *knew* nobody was perfect.

"Ha!" Toby says triumphantly. "Then *neither* of us gets to hang out with Harriet! I'm Hufflepuff."

It looks like I'm going to be wizarding on

my own: given today's behaviour, Nat's clearly Slytherin.

"And, Nicholas," Toby continues, looking more hopeful, "can you prove that in three space dimensions and time, given an initial velocity field, there exists a vector velocity and a scalar pressure field that solves the Navier-Stokes equation?"

Nick shakes his head. "I have no idea what any of that means."

"*Toby*," I interrupt. "That's one of the Millenium Prize Problems. *Nobody* can prove it."

"It has a million-dollar prize," Toby whispers at me urgently. "If he'd known, we could have split the winnings."

I glare at him – I can't believe he's trying to

profit financially from my love life – then turn to Nick in amazement.

Why is he still standing there?

Why hasn't he run away, screaming? Why hasn't he given up and walked away? Why hasn't he sneered, or looked condescending, or laughed at Toby, or judged him for being such a geek?

Or me for being associated with him?

After all, that's what every other boy in school has done for the last ten years. I had a crush on Nick already: but Annabel was right.

Now I really *like* him.

And if he's still here... that must mean he quite likes *me*. Maybe Toby turning up wasn't such a bad thing after al—

"Just one more question," Toby sniffs,

putting the notepad back in his bag and folding his arms in front of him. "Nicholas Hidaka, curly-haired Japanese-Australian supermodel, are you *fully and comprehensively* aware of just how lucky you are right now?"

Yup. Spoke too soon.

Every year, Santa climbs down approximately 91.8 million dark, narrow chimneys. I'm now so utterly humiliated, I'd give anything for just one of them.

A dark hole in the ground would do too: I'm open to suggestions.

"*Toby*," I whimper, staring at the floor while mentally stuffing my bobble hat straight in his mouth, "you can't ask somebody something like—"

"Of course I am," Nick says simply. "Who

doesn't like a girl who knows a full breakdown of jam chart-toppers?"

With a surprised *whoosh* I look up.

He winks at me.

"Then you are a worthy opponent, Nicholas," Toby says in satisfaction. "I shall look forward to our imminent dual to the death, Or maybe just a very aggressive game of chess."

"Ace," Nick grins. "You're on."

He looks at me affectionately in an *are you OK now?* kind of way.

I nod and give a little *I'm OK now* smile back.

Then I metaphorically take the stupid dating list out of my head, crumple it up for the second time this afternoon and throw it back in the bin, where it belongs.

Annabel was right.

This time it's going to stay there.

"I've got to go and make homemade Christmas crackers now," Toby says cheerfully, tightening his satchel straps. "The ones in the shops just never have glass microscope slides in them. Enjoy ice-skating!"

And without further ceremony, Toby leaps down the stairs back into the underground like a little white snowshoe hare: 'Good King Wenceslas' jingling in his wake.

14

There are so many things I need to think about after the last few minutes.

They include:

a) Dungeons & Dragons
b) The Millenium Prize Problem
c) *Ice-skating?*

Only one of those needs dealing with immediately.

"But," I say in surprise, staring up at the stone entrance to the Science Museum, "you said... wasn't there... you told me to..."

Bring gloves.

Oh my God. Nick did not mean *rubber ones.*

Thank goodness I didn't get them out.

"Well, that's the surprise ruined," Nick says wryly, studying my stunned face. "You didn't guess already? I assumed you'd already looked it up on Google, reserved your own skates and maybe written some kind of plan."

Huh. Maybe Nick does know me better than I thought he did.

I just wrote the wrong plan, that's all.

"Well –" I clear my throat indignantly – "I

would have guessed if I'd been given the right *clues*. I don't think you're playing this date properly."

Nick laughs and puts his hands on my shoulders.

A burst of something warm and sweet rushes straight through me: like hot chocolate, or melted marshmallow or a ginger latte. Or something else delicious I suspect I'm going to get very addicted to at some point in the near future.

Then he spins me around and starts walking me in the opposite direction.

This time, I *definitely* know where we're going.

If there's anywhere I've visited almost as much as the Science Museum, it's the building standing directly next to it. Thanks to various movies about dinosaurs, I'm not the only one.

"There," Nick says triumphantly as we turn the corner.

In front of us is the Natural History Museum.

The familiar stone building looms, just as it has since I was tiny: orange terracotta bricks and high spired towers; columns and arches, curves and spikes, like the perfect hybrid of an ancient university college and a traditional fairy-tale castle.

All over it runs the carved menagerie of stone animals I named when I was eight years old: Topaz the monkey; Malachite the parrot; Unikite the fawn, Labradorite and Aventurine the pheasants. (My Year Three school project on semi-precious stones made quite an impression.)

Inside this building is the recently discovered skull of a Barbary lion, caged in the Tower of London 700 years ago. There's a giant butterfly with bullet holes shot through its wings; the first geological map of Britain; a giant squid 8.62 metres long.

The most complete stegosaurus fossil skeleton ever found lives there too, along with the diplodocus that first made me obsessed with dinosaurs.

For me, it's one of the most precious parts of London.

But for the first time in more than a decade, something has changed. What has always been familiar and comfortable territory is suddenly new and fresh again.

As if I've never been here in my life.

As if I'm falling in love with the place all over again.

Lights are everywhere.

The green of the grass has been replaced by an enormous rectangle of white ice, and it's glowing bright purple: criss-crossed with delicate lines like the creases on the palm of a hand.

Round the edges are thousands of tiny fairy lights, wound round the branches of the trees and down the trunks, woven on to the edges of the ice rink like intricate glowing spider's webs. A large carousel shines like a rainbow and spins with little coloured horses: red and blue, yellow and pink, green and orange.

In the middle is an enormous fir tree, covered

in white lights and tiny red baubles, silver bells, gold bows: glittering and nodding sagely.

Frank Sinatra sings 'Have Yourself A Merry Little Christmas'. Violins soar. A piano tinkles.

And dotted around the ice are people.

Giggling and cosy; spinning and holding hands; gliding and laughing and singing.

We know that ice-skating is the oldest human-powered means of transportation on earth. It was invented 3,000 years ago in Finland, when skates were made from animal bones and leather.

But we still don't understand how it works.

Some scientists think pressure from blades causes the top layer of ice to melt. Others believe ice has a naturally unstable layer of molecules that move chaotically across the surface and make it hard to create friction. The only thing most people agree on is that ice is really, really slippery.

I think the people lying all over the floor right now would concur.

I look back at Nick.

His face is shining reflected purple, like an insanely handsome version of Dino from *The Flintstones*.

Honestly, he couldn't have thought of anywhere more perfect to bring me.

But of *all* the things to do on a first date...

Lion Boy chose *slipping*?

He turns slightly anxiously to me and holds out his hands. "Surprise!"

15

Here's the thing I love about people:

We're not like gifts.

You can't hand us to someone, all tied up in a bow and ready to unwrap. It's impossible to open us up and pull everything out; to see who we are all at once.

Or ever, really.

With people, the surprises just keep coming.

*   *   *

As we approach the rink, it's suddenly so cold our breaths have started fogging in front of us like tiny rain clouds.

Our tickets are already reserved, so we pick them up at the front desk, hand them over to a man in yellow gloves and grab our bright blue skates. They're kind of stiff and sticky and they smell like the old teddy my dad stored in the attic for forty years.

We tug them on anyway and start lacing them up in silence.

Nick glances at my flushing face.

"Don't worry," he says with a grin, pulling his black gloves back on. "It's not as hard as it looks."

I push my hands into my red mittens and nod. "Mmm."

"It's just balancing on frozen water, after all. Easy."

I glance through the window at a girl lying on her back in the middle of the rink, waving her arms around like a beetle.

Nick laughs and stands up. "We'll do it together, OK?"

He squeezes my hand and I blink at him, and then at my red mitten. There was something I was just about to tell him, and now I've totally forgotten what it was.

The hot chocolate feeling is back.

Never mind central heating this Christmas: at this rate I'm going to be powering my whole country with the warmth pulsing from my chest cavity.

England will never be cold again.

"Ready?" Nick says as we start staggering awkwardly like penguins in heels towards the rink. "Just stay with me."

And together we step on to the ice.

16

It only takes a few seconds.

With a deep intake of breath, I hold tightly on to the side with both hands and stare at the ice, glowing in front of me.

I exhale hard and watch my breath drift into the air.

Then I let go and start gently moving.

Slowly at first, shifting my weight from one foot to the other. I push my blades into a

V-shape with the heels touching, sliding them slowly out and in again so my feet make a fluid fish shape.

As speed starts to pick up, I bend my knees and do a crossover when I reach the corner: one foot reaching over the other.

Then a one foot glide in a smooth arc

A small hop until I'm facing the other way, pushing backwards across the ice.

A tiny spiral.

And as I begin to really fly – weaving in and out between the other skaters like an otter – I can feel it.

The cold, clean smell. The sharpness of my breath. The whoosh of freezing air against my hot cheeks. The unexpected freedom.

A bubble of lightness.

One that expands inside me until it feels like I'm made of foam: as if I'm about to take one more step and float straight into the air.

I give an abrupt shout of joy.

"Nick!" Beaming, I spin round with a neat little twist and stop with an incredibly satisfying *swoosh*.

A girl directly behind me squeaks in panic, makes a circling movement with her hands and plummets straight to the floor.

Oops.

I help her up apologetically then blink. Nick? I thought he was behind me. He said we'd stay together.

So where exactly *is* he?

I peer in alarm round the rink, and finally see him: still clinging to the side where we started, surrounded by a cluster of similarly positioned people. All splayed against the edges like the little sticky gummy men you throw at walls.

I race back as fast as I can.

"Nick?" I repeat in surprise as he looks up: legs akimbo, face pretty much squidged against the railing. His arms are clamped urgently round the handrails in claw shapes, and every time he tries to find some traction his feet skitter a little further away.

All his normal grace has disappeared, and in its place is awkwardness. Ungainliness. Complete lack of coordination and control.

A vague sense of humiliated panic.

It's like watching a jellyfish abruptly stand up and attempt to go for a long walk before remembering it doesn't actually have any legs.

And it's startlingly familiar.

Just obviously not this way round.

"Hey, Harriet," Nick says, scrambling again and only succeeding in ending up in a slightly different gummy position. "This is fun, isn't it?"

His legs are splayed wide, his cheeks are bright and his woolly hat has slipped down over one eye: all of the black curls on one side of his head are sticking upwards. His nose is red and shiny, his green scarf has unravelled and I've never seen him look so deeply uncool and uncollected.

Or so completely adorable.

"Nick," I say, still shocked, "you can't skate?"

He clears his throat and tries to stand up again. The movement ends up twisting him in a little circle so he's stuck to the side, facing in the opposite direction.

"Apparently not," he says wryly over his shoulder. "It's exactly as hard as it looks. Who knew!"

"Wait – you've never even *been* skating before?"

"I'm from a small town in Australia," he says, wincing up at me. "Not so much ice down there. I kind of assumed I'd be able to pick it up as I went along."

I stare at him in amazement.

I can't believe this.

Is he telling me...

Am I to understand that...

Wait.

Have I got the upper hand in a romantic situation, for the first time ever? Do I get to tell *him* what to do?

Oh my God.

I don't want to sound too smug or triumphant or mean-spirited, obviously.

But this is the *best first date ever.*

With a (completely unnecessary) little hop in the air, I slide confidently in front of Nick and stop with another elaborate *swoosh*. "Here," I say, beaming at him. "Let me help you."

And I hold out my hands.

17

Here's the most romantic Christmas fact I know:

> *In 1913, a couple were fined fifteen dollars for kissing in the streets of New York City on Christmas Day.*

Taking inflation into account, that's $360.31, or £231, just for locking lips during the holidays.

142

I totally understand how that couple over a hundred years ago felt.

Right now I'd consider it an excellent investment.

With every following second that passes, I want to kiss Lion Boy just a little bit more.

He is literally the worst ice skater on the planet.

And I'm including Bambi, an actual lion and a cat I saw crossing a pond on YouTube in that evaluation.

The first time I try to grab his hands, he somehow slides round, clutches at nothing and ends up with a loud *oomph* on his bottom.

"Are you OK?" I ask urgently, bending down.

"Body's intact," Nick grins sheepishly, taking

his hat off and rubbing his increasingly bonkers curls. "Pride may be permanently broken."

Second time, he inexplicably ends up with his face pressed against the barrier and a hand round another guy's ankle.

"Sorry," he mumbles, then clears his throat and jokes: "Can I just say you have *very* nice socks. Are they cashmere?"

He gets shaken off with a prompt *what-the-hell?*

Apparently twenty minutes of laughing is the minimum daily requirement for a long and healthy life.

I'm going to live to three hundred and seven.

By the third attempt – when Nick ends up on the floor with a loud and cartoonish *woah woah wooooooaahh*, accompanied by whirly arms and on-the-spot running – I'm giggling so hard I can't stop an aggressively loud snort from popping out of my mouth.

"Harriet," Nick laughs as I lean over to offer him a hand, "did you just *oink*?"

"No," I snort again, trying unsuccessfully to drag him up off the floor and instead tugging him along the ice like some kind of out-of-control Christmas sleigh. "In Sweden a pig's oink is called a *noff*. Maybe I am *noffing*."

"Or *buu buuing*. That's what it is in Japan."

"*Hunk*, that's Albanian."

"Well, thank you very much," Nick laughs. "You're not so bad yourself, Manners."

We're both giggling so hard now my tummy is starting to hurt, and we have to pause to give us both time to calm down.

Finally.

I've *finally* found a boy who thinks pigs from other countries are as romantic as I do.

With the help of me, another side barrier and a kind passer-by with a larger overall body mass, Nick eventually manages to wobble upright, holding tightly on to both my hands to steady himself.

Then he clears his throat.

"Manners," he says, swaying slightly, "I have a confession. This isn't going as planned *at all*."

"Were you supposed to be swirling me around the rink in a remarkably casual lift by now?"

"Pretty much. And maybe spinning around in a spotlight on my own in the middle, with you watching in rapt admiration."

"Intermittently blowing kisses at an enormous crowd of onlookers?"

"Exactly. And possibly doing really high scissor-kicks randomly at passers-by just to show how simultaneously assertive and flexible I can be."

We both start giggling again.

"Seriously, though," he says, shaking his head and teetering slightly in the process, "I *thought* I was bringing you here because it's romantic."

I glance around us.

Frank Sinatra is still playing softly in the background. The carousel spins. The tree glows. Toffee-apple and cinnamon smells are drifting across the rink, and the little white lights are shining against the ice.

So far, so spot on.

"But –" he coughs – "I'm beginning to wonder whether I *actually* brought you here because deep-down I assumed you'd be bad at ice-skating and I could therefore play the, er… well, hero."

I laugh loudly.

Unusually for me, I know that already. I realised the second I knew we were coming here.

You thought that would happen too, right?

Luckily, thanks to an obsession with Disney on Ice when I was a very young child, I got a year's worth of ice-skating lessons for my birthday and practised every Wednesday night religiously.

OK, I wasn't a *very* young child.

It was eighteen months ago.

The point is: I'm not ridiculous at *every* physical activity ever invented. Just the *vast majority* of them. (Plus obviously I've had little pop-out wheels built into my trainers since I was five: I *knew* they would come in handy one day.)

Nick's expression is now a combination of chagrin, shame and a desire to crawl into the nearest hole in the floor he can find. "I'm a bit of an idiot, aren't I?"

As I said earlier, everyone has the capacity to surprise us.

And that includes Lion Boy.

"Yup," I agree with a broad smile, squeezing his hands. "You are officially an idiot."

For the first time, it feels like we're on equal footing.

Literally. If he goes down now, I do too.

"You were supposed to say no," Nick laughs, squeezing back. "I don't think you're playing this date properly, Harriet."

"Everyone's an idiot sometimes. I'm just glad for once it's you."

Nick shouts with laughter. "I didn't even know *bicepy* was a word."

I playfully lift my chin. "For the record, *Nicholas,* etymologically the *biceps brachii muscle* is where the word for all muscles comes from, because the Latin *musculus* means 'little mouse' and when the arm flexes the bicep it looks just like one. So I stand by what I said."

We both laugh again and stick our tongues out at each other at precisely the same moment.

Then we squeeze hands.

Apparently all the gifts in the 'Twelve Days of Christmas' song would equal 364 separate presents. This moment is so completely perfect, I'd exchange every single one of them to be where I am now.

Although I wouldn't want to spoil it by causing a festive pile-up.

"Come on," I say with a grin, letting go of one hand and turning in an efficient manner to face the ice rink again. We're right in the busiest spot, and two people have already wound up with a crunch on the floor next to us. "Let's skate."

18

I'm not going to lie

I *may* be holding on to Nick's hand slightly longer than I probably have to. We *may* have our shoulders pressed together a little bit closer than is strictly necessary.

His arm *could* be slightly too tightly around my waist for compulsory balance purposes.

What can I say?

Education should be taken *very* seriously.

*   *   *

"Now," I instruct as he wobbles for the umpteenth time, "find your centre of gravity."

I'm trying not to notice the warmth where our fingers are touching. There isn't room in my head for interesting facts about fingertips or nerve endings right now.

I have some giddy floating to attend to.

"Got it," he says, frowning hard and wobbling into a cautious L-shape.

"Stand straight," I suggest, pushing tentatively at the small of his back and trying not to notice another tingle shoot straight through my hand. "You look like you're trying to surf."

"I *am*," he sighs patiently. "That makes infinitely more sense to me. I *significantly* prefer my water in liquid form."

I laugh. "Now keep the blades facing forwards in parallel, apply your weight equally and let me pull you forwards?"

He nods as I start tugging him gently across the ice, like a slightly less broken sleigh.

"Shift your weight from foot to foot as smoothly as you can."

Nick obediently does as he's told.

"Lean forwards and keep the pressure on the blades on the outer ridges."

He follows suit, still staring adorably at his feet with great intensity, as if they're small animals he's never seen before.

"Now blow a raspberry," I command. "And do the funky chicken."

Nick glances up quickly.

Then his face clears and he shouts with

abrupt laughter. That's exactly what he said while guiding me through my first ever fashion shoot in Moscow.

Let's be honest: I'm unlikely to get the upper hand again. This may be the only chance I ever get to pay him back for it.

"I'm afraid I can only manage a strawberry," he says, blowing his tongue out and waggling his arms. "It's really cold."

He grips my hand a little tighter.

Slowly, we start to wobble our way round the glowing rink. Sticking to the sides at first, and then gradually working inwards as he gains confidence.

And as we pick up speed and hit a natural rhythm, I can feel Nick start to relax. With every smooth turn and every neatly timed swish of our feet, I watch his face slowly light up. Just as mine does the first time I learn anything new.

Like the fact that the world's biggest stocking is 106 feet and nine inches long and holds a thousand presents.

Or that approximately three billion Christmas cards are sent every year in the US alone.

Or that the average age of a Christmas tree is fifteen years old.

Which is exactly my age now.

You know what?

Maybe somebody should just prop me up in the corner instead. I'm so happy and sparkling, nobody will be able to tell the difference.

*   *   *

Finally, when we're breathless and worn out with giggling, we slow to a stop by the Christmas tree. Trying to make sure that we're not plonk in the middle of everybody else in the process, obviously.

Frankly, there's romance and there's just getting in the way.

"I've changed my mind," Nick grins triumphantly, wrapping his arms around me. "This was a *genius* idea of mine."

He lost his hat some time ago.

His huge black curls are matted and fluffy, his gloves are soaked, his coat and trousers are still covered in bits of ice and there are little dents in his lips from where he's been biting them so hard in concentration.

So I'm just going to let him have that.

"Speaking of dates," I smile, "where did the girl with pink shoes go? Are we meeting her here?"

"Nope," Nick grins, pulling me a little bit tighter. "Cancelled. How about your date with 'Victor Hugo' tomorrow?"

"Postponed indefinitely." I shake my head. "He died in 1885 so it was really easy to let him down."

Nick laughs loudly, then puts a finger under my chin and lifts it towards him. "We make a good team, Harriet Manners."

And as I stare up at him and catch the lime-green smell that's already starting to feel comfortable – the little mole on his cheek I think I could draw on a map – I realise it's not a question, because we do.

Somehow, we balance each other out.

When Nick slips, I know how to lift him back up. When I panic, he understands how to pick me off the pavement again.

We make each other laugh.

And as I stand on my skate-toes and Lion Boy leans down towards me, it feels as if every Christmas light in London is turning on at once: flickering until I'm covered all over with a million-watt glow.

Because I've suddenly realised there isn't a single embarrassing moment of this story I'd want to change. Every time I've been myself, it's brought me closer to Nick, and all of our differences hold us together.

So even if we wobble, something tells me it'll be OK.

This kiss is just the beginning.

Read on for more geekery...

<u>Harriet's Christmas Day Gift Survey</u>

Dear recipients of gifts from Harriet Manners, please tick the statement that you most closely identify with for each question. Enjoy!

Q1 – How do I feel about this survey?

1.   Thrilled! I've always wanted to give my opinion on gifts in an official yet festive manner.

2.   Daunted. I'm concerned I may get the answers wrong.

3.   Impressed. What a brilliant and original idea!

4.   Productive – I'm so glad I finally get to achieve something real on Christmas Day.

Q2 – What time did Harriet give you your Christmas present?

1. Before 5am: I was shaken awake, which was lovely.

2. Six seconds after the beautiful carols playing downstairs roused me from my slumbers.

3. In the middle of eating Christmas lunch – such a nice distraction!

4. After Harriet, Hugo and Victor got theirs.

Q3 – How did you feel about this time allocation?

1. A little early, but let's get the day started already!

2. Exactly the right time. Harriet assessed my needs perfectly.

3. Too late. I was on tenterhooks all morning.

4. Any time is fine, obviously, because it's Christmas.

Q4 - How was this present wrapped?

1. Mysteriously, and with great care - I had no idea what it was, even after shaking it vigorously.

2. I very much enjoyed the dinosaur wrapping paper because the diplodocuses had little cracker hats on.

3. Poorly - the dog ate the corner off.

4. Too enthusiastically. I'm still making my way through the Sellotape.

Q5 - How did I feel about this present?

1. Ecstatic. How could somebody know my secret hopes and dreams so perfectly?

2. Surprised. I didn't know Harriet had such great taste.

3. A little disappointed that Harriet is the only person in the world who knows me so well because this means my gift-receiving life has now peaked and it's all downhill from here.

4. Worried that my gift to her is nowhere near as good.

Q6 – How do I feel about Harriet as a result?

1. I love her even more.

2. I love her about the same.

3. I love her a little bit less.

4. It makes no difference whatsoever because I love Harriet regardless.

Q7 - Next year, I will be sure to...

1. Not get Harriet yet another copy of a dictionary or encyclopedia she already has.

2. Read the list she gave me a lot more carefully.

3. Hide my gifts to her with more cunning because she found them in November.

4. Stop asking her if this process is totally necessary.

5. Fill in this questionnaire without laughing.

Q8 - Finally, I found this survey...

1. Useful and fun!

2. A fascinating treat to really liven up Christmas evening.

3. A marvellous use of the new pens Harriet has just lent me.

4. Proof that Christmas can be both entertaining and informative.

Merry Christmas!!

Richard's Top Five Christmas Jokes

(as graded by Harriet Manners)

1. Who hides in the bakery at Christmas?

A mince spy!

5/10

2. What do angry mice send to each other at Christmas?

Cross Mouse cards!

4/10

3. What do you get if you eat Christmas decorations?

Tinsilitis!

2/10 Tinsel is spelt with an 'e'

4. What says OH OH OH?

Santa walking backwards!

8/10

5. What does Santa suffer from if he gets stuck down a chimney?

Claus-trophobia

10/10

29/50

Try harder next year, Dad

Minc't Pie

London 1543

Cut the best of fleshe from a Legge of
Mutton, welleth off the bone, and parboyl
until softe. Put it to Suet and rip it small,
adding Salt, Cloves and Mace and spreading
welleth. Take many Currants, clean Prunes,
Raisins and diced Dates and some Orenge-pils
and rub together. When all is goode, put it
into a coffin, or into divers coffins, and bake
until the shade of new corn. When golden,
crack lid open and throw Sugar on top.

Serveth with love.

Verdicts:

Literally the grossest thing I've ever seen – Nat

LOL where did you get the coffin and mace? – Dad

I'm not buying an entire leg of mutton, Harriet. You can have a beef steak – Annabel

Awesome – Toby

Thanks for giving me all of them – Hugo

The HOW WELL DO I KNOW HARRIET MANNERS? Quiz
by Toby Pilgrim

1. What kind of animal is Harriet named after?

Tortoise, although Harriet is significantly faster and less wrinkly.

2. What colour is Harriet's hair, and what colour does she claim it is?

A flaming ruby or a brilliant vermilion: not unlike a glorious sunset over an empty desert or the rosy shade of cochineal dye that comes from the crushed up body of a red beetle.

Strawberry blonde.

3. What does she want to be when she's older?

A palaeontologist, after completing a PHD at Cambridge University, which is only 106.1 miles on the M40 from Oxford University so it will only take me two hours, two minutes to get there by car or three hours by bus.

4. Which country does she want to go to the most?

Myanmar, although this is inaccurate: technically it's still classified as Burma by England.

5. What are her three favourite animals in order of preference?

1. Elephant. 2. Panda. 3. Monkey

I prefer otters.

6. What are her favourite sandwiches?

Chicken and strawberry jam. Which is nowhere near as delicious as banana and Marmite, but I have yet to provide definitive evidence.

7. What's her favourite fact of all time?

There's a molecule in every breath we take that used to be a part of a dinosaur. Wow.

8. Where did she meet Natalie Grey?

Under a piano on the first day of school.
I wish I had been there too.

9. How long have I been stalking her?

Since the second day of secondary school:
that's 1,568 hours so far, and counting.
The first day was a grey, empty wasteland.

10. Who is she definitely going to end up with, romantically?

Toby Pilgrim. It's just a matter of time,
patience and a lot of accurately observed
notes.

11. Why is Harriet Manners so amazing?

She's Harriet Manners.

Harriet's Letter to Santa (aged 5)

Dear Santa,

Hello it's nice to meet you my name is Harriet and I like dogs. I have been practising so I hope you like my letter. How are you I'm fine thank you I tidy my bedroom all the time.

This year I would like

- A ~~thesoorus~~ thesaurus
- A real wand
- A WHITE PUPPY

you remember when I said that I like dogs that was a hint I have drawn a picture so that you get the right one.

Thank you very much I hope you have a nice day I will stay up to meet you.

yours sincerely,

Harriet manners, age 5

PS I left mushrooms because reindeers like them more than carrots

PS2 I left jelly babies because daddy says you like them more than mince pies

xx

Richard's Letter to Santa (aged 35)

DEAR SANTA,

BETWEEN you AND I – fATHER to FATHER – HARRIET'S STANDARD of "tidying" mAy Not Align with A uNIVERSAlly APPRECIATED level of clEANliNESS. But let's ASSUME you hAVE biggER fEStivE fish to fRy At this timE of yEAR.

Now, let's gET down to busiNESS.

FiRstly, don't woRRy About thE PuPPy: it's soRtEd. HE ARRivES ON ChRistmAS EVE, hE's

a white Westie and his name is Hugo.
I'll give you full credit as long as you
don't wake any of us up.

Secondly, I'm struggling with the real
wand request, so if you've got any lying
around please feel free to send one over.
A good one made out of unicorn hair or
phoenix feather, please. We don't need
any dragon heartstrings in this house.

As for me, I would like —

Elizabeth Hurley
A Ferrari
A way of making roast potatoes without
burning them.

Apologies for the early submission. I appreciate it's mid-August, but HARRIET does like to have everything arranged well in advance.

All the best,

Richard MANNERS.

PS Sorry about the jelly babies. They won't be here by the time you arrive.

PPS Neither will the brandy.

Holly Smale's Festive Q & A

What's your favourite Christmas song?

'White Christmas' by Bing Crosby. It's charming and old-fashioned and everything I love about Christmas wrapped up in one song. I played it on repeat while I was writing this story.

What was the main present you always asked Santa for as a child?

Weird fact: I had a massive phobia of Santa as a child. I used to start crying on Christmas Eve because I was so scared of him, and propped a chair against my bedroom door so he couldn't come in. As a result my parents always assured me that my big gifts were coming from them

– not the "horrible old man" – and my sister and I left our stockings in the living room. So Santa and I weren't on speaking terms, unfortunately.

Favourite winter accessory?
Earmuffs and mittens on a string so I don't lose them. And a Terry's Chocolate Orange, to carry with me at all times. Chocolate counts as an accessory if it's round, right?

If you had to watch one Christmas film every single Christmas, which one would you pick?
It's A Wonderful Life, and I *do* watch it every single Christmas. I also read *The Night Before Christmas* every year from a battered up picture

book I've had since I was eighteen months old. Christmas for me is all about tradition and nostalgia.

What would you love to find under the Christmas tree this year?
A round-the-world plane ticket with unlimited stops, please.

What do you love more – wrapping presents or unwrapping presents?
Roughly equal. I'm terrible with my hands – I have no coordination at all – so wrapping presents is a stressful, messy and exhausting process: I have to stick bows all over the ripped bits. But I love the whole ritual of it and the anticipation. Unwrapping is also fun,

but it's over very quickly. I'm a ripper then too.

Which celebrity would you like to meet under the mistletoe?

Jimmy Stewart. As long as I have a time machine as well, obviously.

Would your friends say you're easy to buy for?

I've just asked around: apparently not. In fact, I've just been told I'm a bad combination of particular, mercurial and brutally honest (and I'm a terrible actor). Apparently it's a competition each year to see who can get me a gift I'll *genuinely* like. Sorry, guys.

What's your favourite Christmas memory?

When I was little, my parents would give my younger sister and I a 4am start-time on Christmas morning before we were allowed to wake them up (incredibly generous of them, in hindsight). I remember whispering with her outside the door, obsessively checking the clock and counting down from 100. Then my dad would mumble sleepily, "come on then," and we'd race in and jump on the bed in the dark with our full stockings in our hands. I can still remember exactly how magical and exciting that was, and how happy it made us all.

What's been the best Christmas present you've ever received?

Honestly, I've never really been much of a gift-person. I'm a Christmas baby, so I'd normally get what I wanted for my birthday two weeks beforehand anyway. But the best Christmas gift I've ever received was probably an old, out-of-tune piano I got when I was eight. I heard it being tugged in through the back door while I was opening my stocking, and I thought I was going to explode with happiness. All my dreams of being a (doomed) character in *Little Women* had finally come true.

What goes on top of your Christmas tree?
Our family has an ancient, falling-apart fairy who has been handed down through three generations. She's always wonky, her wings are broken and re-stitched on and the top branch

always looks really uncomfortable. But we all love her anyway.

What would your perfect Christmas Day be?

For me, Christmas is all about family, not gifts. It's about the stories we tell, the jokes, the magic, the lights, the smells, the food. It's about making peppermint creams with my mum and going on long snowy walks with my dad and dancing round the living room to festive music with my sister and her puppies. I've only ever spent one Christmas on my own, and I wouldn't choose to do it again. As long as the people I love are there, I'm happy.

What would you give Harriet as a Christmas present?

Lion Boy. So – with this story – that's what I've done. ☺

Read on for a bonus **GEEK GIRL** story…

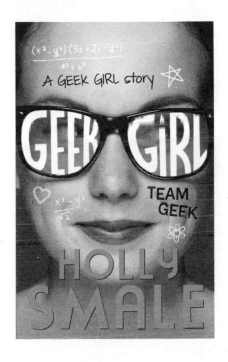

geek/giːk/h noun informal, chiefly N. Amer.

1 an unfashionable or socially inept person.

2 an obsessive enthusiast.

3 a person who feels the need to look up the word 'geek' in the dictionary.

DERIVATIVES *geeky* adjective.

ORIGIN from the related English dialect word *geck* 'fool'.

My name is Harriet Manners, and here are some things I love:

1. Documentaries about king penguins narrated by David Attenborough.
2. Getting a Q *and* a U in Scrabble.
3. Knowing that you can fit a baby through the blowhole of a whale.
4. Wondering if anybody has actually tried.
5. Putting things I love in lists.

Here are some things I'm not so keen on:

1. Having heavy things intentionally thrown at my face.

2. Running, jumping, catching, or any other activity that requires breath regulation and limb control.
3. Getting my furry legs out.
4. Public humiliation (see points 1, 2 and 3).
5. Anything that involves the word "wing" that doesn't feature penguins or aviation.

Suffice to say, I'm not super happy that today's PE class is netball. In the course of an average lifetime we accidentally eat seventy assorted insects and ten spiders, and I'd rather have them all in one mouthful right now.

Sadly that's not an option we've been given.

"Girls," Miss Watkins says sharply as Nat and I slink miserably out of the changing room. "It's a bit of rain. It's not going to kill you."

"That's not *necessarily* true," I point out

as we shuffle past, tugging at our tiny nylon skirts to make them a bit more respectable. (In my case, longer; in my best friend's case, a more flattering shape.) "Floods are the most widespread natural disaster apart from wildfires, and can cause walls of water up to 20 feet high. Rain *literally* kills thousands of people a year all over the world."

"*Exactly*," Nat agrees enthusiastically. "I hope you're insured, Miss. I hope you can sleep at night, risking our lives like this."

My Best Friend and I have very few things in common, but a mutual hatred of PE is one of them.

"That's very kind of you, Natalie," Miss Watkins says smoothly. "I do indeed sleep very well. I have a brand-new air-sprung mattress and it's extremely comfortable. You should look into getting one."

Nat scowls, and I clear my throat and start walking faster so we can keep up. I can already tell from the speed of Miss Watkin's stomping and the shape of her shoulders that next week's Parent-Teachers' Evening is going to be an interesting one.

"I'm really sorry Nat and I were late," I mumble. "It was entirely unintentional and a result of a timetable error and a directional miscalculation."

"You could say *late*," our PE teacher states flatly, without turning around. She speeds up slightly. "Or you could say *hiding in the stationery cupboard*."

Nat and I glance at each other in guilty silence. She's absolutely right: that's exactly where we were. At least until a very tiny Year Seven girl opened it and started screaming because she thought we were waiting in there to kill her with sharpened pencils.

In our defence, two words: *netball* and *raining*.

"Well, you're here now." Miss Watkins

gives us a glance of pure vengeance, and then pushes open the door to the playground and our punishment. "I'll leave you to explain to the rest of the class why they've been waiting for you both in the freezing rain, shall I?"

She points to where a group of miserable girls are standing, huddled in a silent group around an orange ball and dripping wet, just like Attenborough's penguins.

Sugar cookies. They were supposed to start without us.

Actually, scrap that. They were supposed to start without us and play the entire game without us and finish without us. That was kind of the point.

"Harriet," Nat says in a low voice as Miss Watkins blows her whistle to stop them all muttering and picks a large pile of orange and green bibs off the floor. "We should probably start hoping for that twenty-foot tidal wave."

Because in the middle of the group – freezing,

soaked to the bone and looking absolutely furious – is the third word in our defence:

Alexa.

So, imagine you're in a rainforest.

It's such an enormous rainforest it feels as if there's no way out, and sometimes – in the darkest parts where it gets really thick and overwhelming – when you look up you can't even see sunlight. All you can see are trees and rainforest spreading in every direction all around you forever and ever, with no end in sight. And you can't imagine what it's like not being in the rainforest.

Well, that's what school is like.

There are all kinds of animals here: monkeys and toucans and anteaters and sloths and butterflies. All just swinging and flying and eating and sleeping and trying to get through the day as best they can. Minding their own business. Trying not to get eaten.

I'm like a polar bear. Lost, bewildered and incapable of fitting in. Unsure of what to do, or how I got here, or how on earth to get out again.

The majority of the group in front of us right now are the tigers. The jaguars; the anacondas; the baboons; the poison dart frogs and piranhas. These animals don't just belong here: they rule here. You tread as softly as possible so you don't disturb them; you keep your ankles covered and your head protected. You stay quiet and hope with every bit of you they choose something else to rip apart. It's not fair, but it's the rule of the jungle. There's no point in complaining. It's just the way it is.

Alexa's the mosquito. Small and sneaky, and by far the most dangerous.

And always, always wanting blood.

All Nat and I wanted today was to stay out of the way: warm, dry and unnoticed. Instead, we've managed to make everything a billion times worse.

Which – if you know me – is not a massive and unprecedented surprise.

"Captains," Miss Watkins says sharply, nodding at what I can now see is two distinct groups of sodden girls. Alexa and Becky obediently step forward. "Choose your players quickly. Alexa first."

Nat may hate netball, but she's naturally fast and strong, and when a ball flies at her face her automatic reaction is to catch it. Not flinch, cry out and cover her eyes with her hands, which is how I play any kind of sport.

I start to shuffle towards Becky.

"Harriet," Alexa says.

I keep walking, because obviously all the Year Seven screaming has damaged my hearing.

"Harriet," Alexa says again, more loudly. "I choose Harriet Manners."

There are loud murmurs from both teams.

"You realise the point of a game is to *win*, right?" one of Alexa's minions says.

Alexa shrugs and casts a furtive look at Miss Watkins. "Harriet deserves a chance, right? Maybe she'll surprise us all and pull it out of the bag."

OK: Alexa has hated me since we were five years old. And at no stage whatsoever at any part of the last decade a) has she given me a chance, or b) have I pulled anything out of the bag.

I'm not even totally sure where the bag is, or what's supposed to be inside it.

"That's a lovely attitude, Alexandra," Miss Watkins says approvingly.

"Fine," Becky says after a puzzled silence, shaking her head. "I'll take Nat, then."

Nat gives me a look that says What The Hell Is Going On? and then strides over to the other side of the pitch and pulls a green bib over her head.

"Here," Alexa says, handing me a bright orange one and inexplicably saying nothing about how it matches my hair.

I blink and hand it back. "I think it's the wrong one. This is Goal Attack."

"Good luck, Manners." Alexa shoves it back at me then starts walking on to the middle of the netball pitch. "You're going to need it."

My hands are starting to shake. I'm normally forced into the passive/loser position of Goal Keeper, and then spend most of my time staring at a tree in the distance, working out what kind of clouds they are behind it and being yelled at to WAKE UP, HARRIET by Goal Defence just before a ball gets lobbed at my head.

What the sugar cookies is Alexa doing? Is she *that* desperate to impress Miss Watkins? Does she know I'll fail horribly, and that's what she wants?

Or has she had a sudden, abrupt change of heart about me and wants to offer me the world's weirdest, netball-shaped olive branch?

But there isn't time to work it out, so I swallow, pull the bib over my head and walk to my unfamiliar position on the court.

And the whistle blows.

According to Wikipedia, the origins of netball can be traced back to a women's version of basketball, created in 1891. Back then, the ladies wore floor-length dresses and hats and tossed the ball gently and probably said things like "how absolutely spiffing" when they scored a goal.

I really wish it was still like that.

The court is a battleground: girls are screaming, yelling, jumping, elbowing, running, spinning; whistles are blowing; the ball seems to be in six places at once. I'm disorientated within five seconds.

All I know – according to what is being yelled at me – is I have to FOCUS ON THE BALL, so that's what I'm doing. I'm focusing so hard, I can't see anything else. I feel like I'm at an opticians and they're waving a pencil in front of my nose: the rest of the court is a total blur with an orange spot in the middle.

"Harriet!" somebody shouts.

"Anna!"

"Over here!"

"No – to me!"

"Catch it, Fiona!"

"HARRIET!"

Hannah in a green bib grabs the ball to my left, and passes it to Fiona on my right. Then it gets thrown over my head to my left again to Ellen, and 90 degrees to my right. Anna runs in one direction for a few steps, grabs it then lobs it; Lucy steps in and throws it over my head yet again, where Jo snatches it and passes it to Nat.

And all I'm doing is backing down the pitch, spinning in little circles, following the ball, like a kitten chasing a mouse on the end of a bit of string.

"HARRIET!" somebody shouts loudly as I dizzily try to stabilise myself. "GRAB IT!"

Suddenly I can see an orange circle, flying straight at my face. I close my eyes and put my hands out, and – to my absolute shock – the ball sticks.

I open them again and look at it in total astonishment. The way a father looks at a newborn child: as if they can't believe they haven't dropped it already.

"NOW SCORE!" Alexa screams, pointing at the hoop above me.

This is it, I suddenly realise.

This is my metamorphosis. This is the bit where everything could change: where I transform from outsider Geek – incapable of touching her own toes without sitting on a chair first – to Bouncy Athlete Extraordinaire.

They'll make me Captain of the netball team. I'll suddenly know how to crowd surf and dance. I'll get invited to parties where everybody knows the words to the same songs even though they're not written down anywhere.

I take a deep breath. People are shouting, screaming, yelling: there are bodies everywhere, and feet, and ponytails, and the ball feels gritty and rough in my hands.

I'm going to prove Alexa right: I'm going to surprise everyone. Whether that's what she was intending or not.

The shouting gets louder and louder, a celebratory whistle is piercing through the air, and all I can feel is a triumphant pulse of blood in my head as nobody makes even the smallest effort to grab it off me.

Which means I can do this.

I hold the ball carefully above my head. Then I take another deep breath, aim, close my eyes and shoot.

For a few fractions of a second there's nothing but silence. Nothing but quietness, and darkness, and rain. Then I open my eyes, just in time to see the orange ball, sailing through the hoop.

Which means I just scored the first goal of my entire life. The first *anything*.

"YESSSSSS!!!" I squeak, jumping up and down. What does my dad shout when he's watching football? "BACK OF THE NET! Or – you know – through it!"

And I turn to high-five Nat, even though she's on the other team.

Except she's not there.

For a few seconds I hold my hand in the air, waiting for the praise and adulation and cheering, and it's only then I realise the court's still strangely silent. Silent, and wet, and there's a crowd of girls in orange and green, staring at me.

Then I see Nat's face – somewhere in the

distance – hidden in her hands, and Alexa's expression. It's pure, incandescent triumph.

And the whistle is still blowing.

A shrimp's heart is in its head, and I suddenly feel like I might be turning into one: my cheeks are pounding and beating and heating and racing, as if they're about to explode.

It's the wrong goal.

That's why nobody was trying to stop me. That's why everybody was shouting. That's why Miss Watkins is going crazy with her whistle. That's why I'm stood next to the Goal Keeper of my own team, looking like a total plonker. Because I was running in the wrong direction.

The direction Alexa pointed me in.

"*Disqualified*," Miss Watkins shouts, blowing her whistle for the millionth time. "Free penalty to the opposition." The entire green team – bar Nat – suddenly explodes into triumphant shouts and push forward Hannah, who has never, ever missed a penalty shot in PE history. The orange team explodes too, but in the opposite way.

"*Idiot*," somebody shouts.

"What a *total geek*," somebody else yells.
"Miss! That's unfair! Harriet's obviously too
stupid to play!"

"Seriously, what is *wrong* with her?"

"She wasn't even *allowed* in that section!
She should have been stopped! Miss, that's
cheating! She's a mole for the other team!"

My cheeks are burning, my eyes are stinging,
and all I want to do is run away. But I can't,
because I've already done that once today and I
obviously wasn't very good at it.

"I'm really sorry," I say, looking desperately
around me for something to make it better.

"Such a shame," Alexa says, shaking her
head and taking the bib off me. "I was really
rooting for you, Harriet. How about you take
Goal Keeper instead, since you're so keen on
the other team's goal?"

I stare at her, and then at the rainforest

behind her: all snarling and snickering and squeaking and jibbering. Furious and disgusted with me. Ready to attack. Alexa just risked losing an entire game to make them hate me. That was her revenge for making her soggy and cold: ritual humiliation.

Although, in fairness, even *she* couldn't have realised I'd be *that* stupid. I might as well have covered myself in gravy and handed myself to her on a plate with a sprinkling of rosemary on my head.

I nod quietly and take the bib off her.

"Hey – it's the same colour as your hair," she adds, laughing and heading back to the centre of the court.

The whistle blows again, and the game starts. Except this time I'm on the edge of it: standing uselessly by the same goal, with my hands stuck in the air, staring into the distance. A polar bear again.

Hannah gives her team-mates a quick wink,

and then lobs the ball through the net with the grace of a performing seal.

As the entire rainforest erupts again, I glance quickly at Nat. She grins, shrugs and makes an enormous wave motion with her hand.

And, as I grin back, I can feel us both thinking the same thing:

We're going to have to find a better cupboard.

Acknowledgements

Thanks to my mum, for always making Christmas magical: you've given me so many special memories. Thanks to my sister, for energetically sharing them with me, and Dad, for getting up early enough to join in.

Thanks to my Grandma and Grandad, who have always hosted Christmas so graciously and with such fabulous roast potatoes.

Finally, thanks to Kate Shaw, Ruth Alltimes, Lizzie Clifford and the rest of Team Geek: for encouraging me to finally tell this story.

I can't think of a better way of celebrating.

Thank you. x

See how it all began...

Harriet Manners knows a lot of things.

* Cats have 32 muscles in each ear
* Bluebirds can't see the colour blue
* The average person laughs 15 times per day
* Peanuts are an ingredient in dynamite

But she doesn't know why nobody at school seems to like her. So when she's offered the chance to reinvent herself, Harriet grabs it. Can she transform from geek to chic?

The geek is back!

Harriet Manners also knows:

* Humans have 70,000 thoughts per day
* Caterpillars have four thousand muscles
* The average person eats a ton of food a year
* Being a Geek + Model = a whole new set of graffiti on your belongings

But clearly she knows nothing about boys. And on a whirlwind modelling trip to Tokyo, Harriet would trade in everything she's ever learnt for just the faintest idea of what she's supposed to do next...

Geek girl goes Stateside...

Harriet Manners knows a lot of facts:

* New York is the most populous city
in the United States
* Its official motto is 'Ever Upward'
* 27% of Americans believe we never
landed on the moon

But she has no idea about modelling Stateside. Or,
even more importantly, what to do when the big
romantic gestures aren't coming from her boyfriend...

The original geek returns...

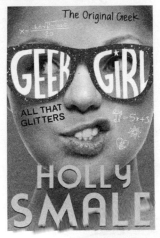

The Original Geek

GEEK GIRL

ALL THAT GLITTERS

HOLLY SMALE

Harriet Manners has high hopes for the new school year: she's a Sixth Former now, and things are going to be different. But with Nat busy falling in love at college and Toby preoccupied with a Top Secret project, Harriet soon discovers that's not necessarily a good thing...

No. 1 Geek!

Harriet Manners knows almost every fact there is.

* She knows duck-billed platypuses
don't have stomachs
* She knows that fourteen squirrels were
once detained as spies
* She knows only one flag in the
world features a building

And for once, Harriet knows exactly how her life should go. She's got it ALL planned out. So when love is in the air, Harriet is determined to Make Things Happen! If only everyone else would stick to the script...

Has GEEK GIRL overstepped the mark, and is following the rules going to break hearts all over again?

DO NOT MISS...

The sixth and FINAL GEEK GIRL!

COMING SOON

GEEK G★RL

HEAD TO OUR FACEBOOK PAGE

f /GeekGirlSeries

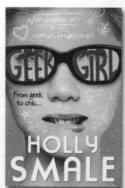

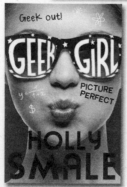

 @HolSmale